THE TALE OF THE SLY MONGOOSE

BIANCA AND THE ANGUILLA ISLAND ADVENTURES ™

2021 First Paperback Edition
Copyright © 2021 The Journey Productions, LLC
Copyright © Text and Illustrations The Journey Productions, LLC

The Journey Productions, LLC
Published by The Journey Productions, LLC
1175 Marlkress Road, Unit 4645
Cherry Hill, New Jersey 08034
www.JenniferLewisHall.com

Library of Congress Cataloging-in-Publication Data

Lewis-Hall, Jennifer.
The Tale Of The Sly Mongoose Bianca And The Anguilla Island Adventures (TM) / Jennifer Lewis-Hall ; illustrated by Kofi Johnson.
p. cm.
ISBN: 9798799744069

Happy Reading!

Jennifer Lewis Hull

ACKNOWLEDGMENT

For my sons Joseph and Joshua and children and families everywhere who love a great adventure A special thank you to my husband Rick and my family and friends.

To my beloved angels - grandmother Bianca, grandfather Joel, mother Evelyn, father Arthur - and all my ancestors - I rise, we rise on your wings. I am because of you. With all my heart I thank you for sharing so much about our history and life on this magical beautiful island of Anguilla. To my family, I love you.

The Anguilla sun was shining brightly through Bianca's window. A balmy bay breeze blew her tattered curtains up and then down. The wind rattled her shutters just a bit: tat-tah-tat-tat, tat-tah-tat-tat.

She reached down to where Bea lay in bed and gently pushed the curly braids out of Bea's eyes. "Time to get up and rattle dem coconut trees."

That was mother's way of saying it was time for Bea to do her chores – all of them, before she could swim in Meads Bay and pick shells for a necklace or make funny footprints in the sand. Bea loved adventures and she loved to play. But today was not a playing day.

Her mother spoke softly but sternly as she listed Bea's chores. "Don't let any grass grow under your feet me dear, de time is flying by. First, ya must help your big brother Gabe pick de ripest coconuts you can find. Next, help your Auntie Alice shell dem pigeon peas for tomorrow's dinner. After dat, it's time to hang the clothes on the line."

"So remember, Bea," her mother said. "Rattle dem trees, sh[...] dem peas, and when you put the clothes on the line, please m[...] dear – do not whine."

"Oh," she added. "Me want to tell you one more ting. Steer clear of Mr. Hodges' mongoose – he's a sly one."

Bea yawned. "Sly how?" she wondered to herself. "He's just a teeny, tiny mongoose who hangs out in the trees."

Little Bea had a big attitude. Sitting on the porch with her face in an angry pout, she thought, "If I can just get someone else to do my chores, my day will be just fine."

She frowned and poked her lips out. "I could sneak and ask my brother Jimmie to help out, but he's getting ready for the boat races," she mumbled. "I know Jo-el from West End fancies me, and his sistah Aggy would do anything me want. Or there's my friend Cedric up the road, I could call on him."

But Bea remembered her mother's words. Could any of her friends 'rattle dem trees, shell dem peas and remember not to whine' while putting th clothes on the line?

"No," Bea thought. "It's just too much work." She flung an old sock from the wash bucket onto the clothes line.

There must be someone else, someone who could do the chores just the way mother liked them – and someone who wouldn't tell. Then, as Bea sat under the grape tree shielding herself from the hot afternoon sun, she heard something scurrying beneath the brush.

"What's that noise?" Bea wondered. "It must be my old goat Rufus, the one with gray whiskers and a big belly." But Rufus was quietly munching grass in his shady spot under a tree.

Slowly, quietly, Bea picked up a coconut with one hand, and as silently as she could, she peeked between the leaves.

Suddenly and with lightning speed, there was Mr. Hodges' scruffy old mongoose poking his head through the brush. He was the very mongoose her mother had warned her about.

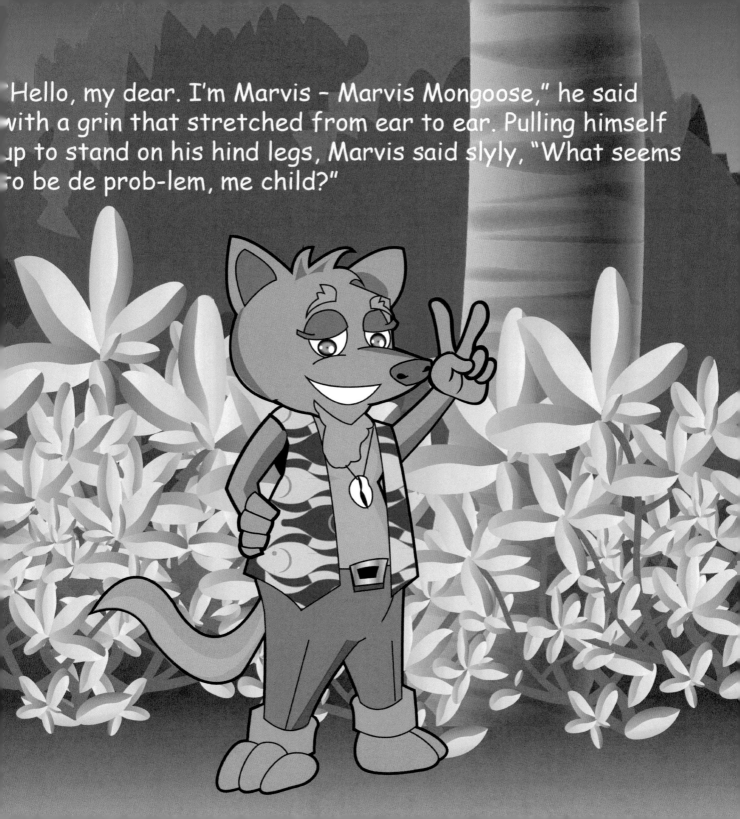

"Hello, my dear. I'm Marvis – Marvis Mongoose," he said with a grin that stretched from ear to ear. Pulling himself up to stand on his hind legs, Marvis said slyly, "What seems to be de prob-lem, me child?"

"Oh!" Bea yelped and backed away from the brush. "My mother told me not to share a word wid you."

"Who, me? Marvis, Marvis the Magnificent Mongoose?" He opened his eyes wide and smiled a slow smile. "I heard you talking to yourself by de coconut tree – vexin' 'bout all the things you have to do. I'm the one who can help you rattle dem trees, shell dem peas and put the clothes on the line."

With a wink, he added, "And a mongoose doesn't whine."

Little Bea's heart jumped. If she wanted to make it to Meads Bay today, she would need help with her chores. And oh, how she wanted to swim and pick shells and make funny footprints in the sand.

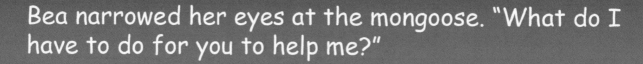

Bea narrowed her eyes at the mongoose. "What do I have to do for you to help me?"

"Oh, nothing much," said Marvis Mongoose. Then, rubbing his hungry belly and grinning his wide grin, he added, "There is one ting you could do for a mongoose on the loose. I'll need... just a few tings." He blinked a slow blink. Bea waited.

"Come by me with your sun bonnet, your apron for pickin' peas and the sack that dem use for catching those beautiful coconuts off de trees," said the mongoose. "I'll be right here when you get back. Right here rattlin' de trees, shellin' the peas and putting the clothes on the line. And I promise not to whine."

Little Bea skipped down the rocky road, past her grandmother's house on South Hill and round the roundabout heading away from the Valley. She walked fast and she walked slow. She walked and walked and walked. Finally, she smelled the saltwater air and she felt the breeze of the bay blowing back her braids.

Bea giggled when she reached Meads Bay. "I have all day to play!" she thought. She swam and dragged her feet in the sand and sifted through the blue waters in search of shells.

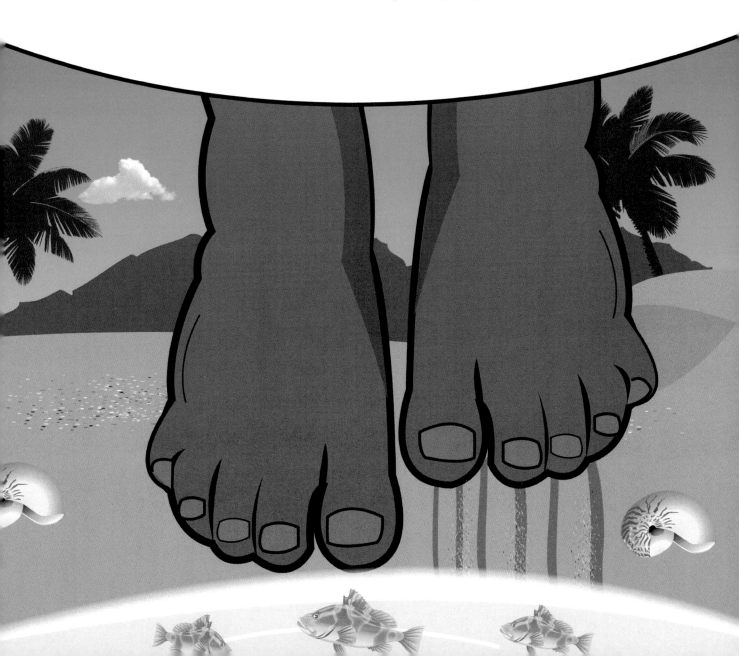

She picked and she plucked until she found a silver and blue shell that she could put on a piece of twine and wear around her neck.

The afternoon passed and Bea began to get hungry and sleepy. When the sun turned dark orange like the skin of the overripe mangos behind her Auntie's house, it was time to go home. "Mr. Sun, done come. Me feel like I could reach up and touch you," she said. "But since you're the color of a giant orange sweet fruit in the sky, it's time for me to say bye-bye."

Little Bea ran most of the way home. On and on and on she ran. She ran and ran back around the roundabout, back past her grandmother's house and back down her family's rocky road.

"Whew!" Bea let out a big sigh when she reached home. She rested her tired feet on an old dried piece of coral. But as quickly as a fierce wind rolls off the sea, she remembered the mongoose.

"Now, where is that mongoose on the loose?" she wondered. "He'd better be done rattlin' the trees, shellin' the peas, putting the clothes on the line and remembering not to whine. I don't want to get into trouble."

But Marvis was nowhere in sight. The sly mongoose had disappeared - and so had the food for tomorrow night's dinner. There were no coconuts cut from the trees and no shells with peas. There were no clothes on the line. Bea began to whine.

Instead, she heard her own name in the distance. "Bea, Bea!" It was her mother. Bea winced. "Bea, come!" mother called. Little Bea dragged her salt-covered feet, the feet that had played in the sand and swam in the bay instead of walking Bea along on her chores.

"Bea," her mother asked, "Did you rattle dem trees, shell dem peas and put the clothes on the line?" She looked hard into Bea's eyes. "You promised me, child, you would not whine!"

Bea held her head so low her braids fell into her face. "No, Mom." She took a deep breath. "The mongoose, Mr. Hodges' mongoose – Marvis. He promised he would help."

"The same mongoose, Bea, that I warned you 'bout?"

Bea looked down at her sandy feet. "Yes," she said, her voice cracking. "And now we have nothing to eat for tomorrow's dinner."

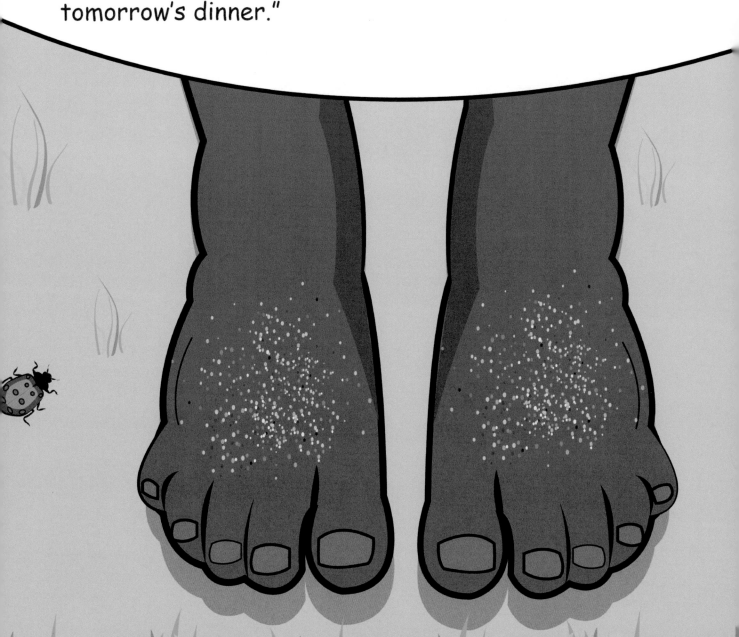

"Little Bea," her mother said, reaching for Bea's hand, "let this be a lesson: you mustn't disrespect your parents. The sly mongoose will beat you at his game every time. When I warned you about him, I warned you for your own good."

"I know, Mom," Bea said softly. "I'm sorry. It was up to me to do my chores, not somebody else. Like you say, we all have to have responsibilities." Bea's mother gave her hand a warm squeeze.

At that very moment the mongoose was waddling down the road wearing Bea's hat and apron, his belly full of coconut milk and peas. Who should he meet but his fiercest enemy – the cobra, just as fast as he was.

Marvis tried his nifty new disguise. "Oh, Mr. Cobra," he said in his best little girl voice. "Please excuse me, I'm not a mongoose at all, you see." But the cobra could see Marvis' long furry tail beneath his apron, and the cobra felt lean and mean. He was not weighed down by a belly full of coconut milk.

The cobra looked closely at Marvis as his bonnet slid to one side. Out popped a mongoose ear. Marvis gulped. "I'm still just as fast as always," he said with a weak grin.

Speaking in a deep voice as he slowly uncoiled his long body, the cobra replied, "Hand over the coconuts." The mongoose whimpered. "And the peas."

Marvis remembered sheepishly how he was supposed to rattle dem trees and shell dem peas, put the clothes on the line and remember not to whine. Now he was the one whining as he reluctantly handed over the food he had stolen from Bea.

Meanwhile, Bea and her mother walked hand-in-hand toward the sea in search of tomorrow night's dinner. Soon they reached the bend in the road where the mongoose and the cobra were arguing – right where they had dropped the sack of coconuts and the pot of peas. It had taken just an instant for the cobra to realize that there was no way for a snake to break the coconuts, drink the milk or even eat the pigeon peas.

Bea tiptoed past Marvis and Mr. Cobra and used her mother's apron to gather up the coconuts. Her mother picked up the delicious pot of peas, placing it gently atop her head just like Bea's grandmother did.

Looking down at Bea, her mother said in a soft voice, "You made a mistake today, little Bea, but you were a big girl by admitting what you did wrong and doing your very best to fix it."

She bent down to hug Bea tight. "Next time, you'll remember to rattle dem trees, shell dem peas, put the clothes on the line -"

"- and remember not to whine," Bea finished with a smile.

Together they set off down the rocky road with tomorrow night's dinner.

THE END

FUN WORDS

Here is a fun game. Grab your dictionary and look for these words and write the definition on the lines provided.

Sly

_____
_____
_____

Mongoose

_____
_____
_____

Billy Goat

_____
_____
_____

Cobra

_____
_____
_____

Responsibility

_____
_____
_____

Continued on next page.

Moral

_____

_____

_____

Coral

_____

_____

_____

Bay

_____

_____

_____

Character

_____

_____

_____

THEMES IN THE TALE OF THE SLY MONGOOSE

Honesty, Responsibility, Respect, Forgiveness, Caribbean Life,
Environment and Culture, Conflict, Resolution and Decision Making.

FLAG OF ANGUILLA

FUN FACTS ABOUT ANGUILLA

Island name: Anguilla (AV). The name means eel in Spanish and Italian.
Country: Anguilla (British overseas territory).
Nationality: Anguillan(s).
Language: English (official).
Island's Capital: The Valley.
Population: 16,000 (2014).
Climate: Tropical
Coastline: 61 km.

Summary: An adventurous and curious girl on the Caribbean island of Anguilla is faced with doing her chores and is distracted by a sly mongoose.

About The Tale Of The Sly Mongoose

The Tale Of The Sly Mongoose - Bianca And The Anguilla Island Adventures is the story of an adventurous and curious girl named Bianca living on the beautiful Caribbean island of Anguilla in the British West Indies. Bianca loves to play on the breathtakingly enchanting beaches with turquoise blue water where she can pick shells and wiggle her toes in the sand. She is faced with some decisions she has to make when it comes to doing her chores and keeping up with her responsibilities. The very convincing sly mongoose makes it all the more difficult as he uses some of his classic tricks to distract her. Part folktale and part historical the story takes the reader on some twists and turns and delightful sun-filled adventures as this young adventurer thinks about her choices and learns some important life lessons. Based on the author's grandparents as children on the island and her own love of Anguilla, The Tale Of The Sly Mongoose is a story filled with surprises, fun things to learn and experience.

About The Author

Network television journalist, motivational speaker and author Jennifer Lewis-Hall has built an exceptional career in network and local television as well as multimedia with a focus on raising awareness about many issues impacting our communities including education and literacy. Her own love of books and sharing empowering and positive information has lead Lewis-Hall to write three books – the latest of which is this children's book "The Tale Of The Sly Mongoose - Bianca And The Anguilla Island Adventures." Part folktale and part historical the story takes the reader on some twists and turns and delightful sun-filled adventures as the main character Bianca, a young adventurer, thinks about her choices and learns some important life lessons. Based on the author's grandparents as children on the island and her own love of Anguilla, The Tale Of The Sly Mongoose is a story filled with surprises, fun things to learn and experience. She is also the author of books focusing on work, career and family - "Life's A Journey – Not A Sprint" and "Life Changes: Using The Power of Change To Transform Your Life." Jennifer is a graduate of Northwestern University's Medill School of Journalism and has a bachelor's degree from Douglass College at Rutgers University. In recognition of her professional accomplishments, board service and community involvement this Emmy-nominated journalist has received numerous awards including the 2021 Camden County Freedom Medal Award.

Made in the USA
Middletown, DE
13 April 2022

63831318R00031